# Elmo **Loves** You!

# Elmo Loves You!
## A Poem by ELMO

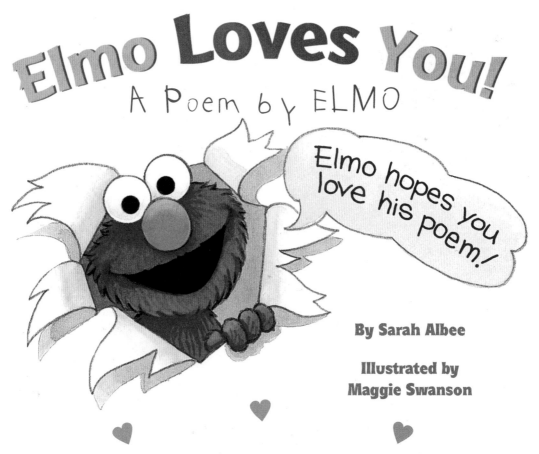

Elmo hopes you love his poem!

**By Sarah Albee**

**Illustrated by Maggie Swanson**

The DALMATIAN PRESS and PIGGY TOES PRESS names and logos are trademarks of Dalmatian Publishing Group, Atlanta, Georgia 30329. No part of this book may be reproduced or copied in any form without written permission from the copyright owner. All rights reserved.

Printed in Dongguan, Guangdong, China

10  11  12  13  SF  36041 10  9  8  7  6  5  4  3  2  1
Sesame Street Handle Box Set Book: Elmo Loves You!

Everyone loves something.
Babies love noise.
Birds love singing.

Kids love toys.

Bert loves pigeons,
and pigeons love to coo.
Can you guess who Elmo loves?
Elmo loves *you!*

Piggies love to roll in mud.

Penguins love the snow.

Farmers love to wake up early.
Roosters love to crow.

Zoe loves the library. Grover loves it, too.
Elmo whispers quietly, "Elmo loves *you!*"

The Count loves counting things.

How does Elmo love you? Let me count the ways!

Ernie loves to drum.

Monsters love to exercise.

Kids love bubble gum.

Natasha and her daddy love playing peekaboo.
But—*psssst!*—before you turn the page...
Elmo loves *you!*

Everyone loves something.
Elmo told you this was true.
And now you know who Elmo loves:
Elmo loves *you!*

Before Elmo ends his poem,
Elmo wants to ask you this:
Will you be Elmo's valentine?
Can Elmo have a kiss?

What are some things that you love?